Scholastic Publications Ltd.,
10 Earlham Street, London WC2H 9RX, UK

Scholastic Inc.,
730 Broadway, New York, NY 10003, USA

Scholastic Tab Publications Ltd.,
123 Newkirk Road, Richmond Hill,
Ontario L4C 3G5, Canada

Ashton Scholastic Pty. Ltd.,
P O Box 579, Gosford, New South Wales,
Australia

Ashton Scholastic Ltd.,
165 Marua Road, Panmure, Auckland 6,
New Zealand

First published by Scholastic Publications Limited, 1988
Text copyright © John Cunliffe, 1988
Illustrations copyright © Scholastic Publications Limited and
Woodland Animations Limited, 1988

ISBN 0 590 70999 2

Made and printed in Hong Kong
Typeset in Times Roman by AKM Associates (UK) Ltd,
Ajmal House, Hayes Road, Southall, London

Postman Pat
and the
Letter-Puzzle

Story by **John Cunliffe** *Pictures by* **Joan Hickson**
From the original Television designs by **Ivor Wood**

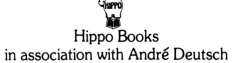

Hippo Books
in association with André Deutsch

"Just look at those leaves," said Pat. "Turning brown already. We'll soon be thinking of Christmas."

Pat was on his way with his letters. Jess was in his basket at Pat's side. He wasn't thinking of Christmas. He was thinking of rabbits. He had just seen two fat ones, running across the school field. The road was busy in Greendale this morning.

Pat met Sam Waldron with his mobile shop,
Peter Fogg on his tractor, Dr Gilbertson
in her red Sierra, George Lancaster in his
milk van, Ted Glen driving the Greendale
bus, and the mobile library.

"It's getting as busy as Pencaster," said
Pat. "And look at all these letters and
packets. It's going to be a busy day."

By the time Pat got to Greendale
Farm, Mrs Pottage and the twins had got
their new books from the mobile library.
Mrs Pottage was in the basket chair by
the fire, and Katy and Tom were lying on
the floor, all reading their books.
Baby Paul was playing with his woolly
monkey.

"Now then," said Pat, "noses in books
at this time of day? What about the
washing-up?"

"Oh, never mind the washing-up," said Mrs Pottage. "We've just got some lovely books from the library, and the washing-up can wait till I finish this story."

"Well, you won't have time for these letters," said Pat.

"Just put them on the table," said Mrs Pottage. "They can wait as well."

"And what are the twins busy reading?" said Pat. "They're very quiet this morning. Let's see? Horses. Both reading about horses!"

"Don't you know why?" said Katy. "That's because . . ."

"Because we've got . . ." said Tom.

". . . a pony," said Katy.

"Of our very own," said Tom.

"And . . ." said Katy.

". . . Peter's going to teach us to ride," said Tom.

"And it's lovely," said Katy.

"Come and see it," said Tom.

"Quick!" said Katy. "Come on, Pat."

"Well . . ." said Pat.

"It's only in the bottom meadow," said Tom. "Behind the barn."

"It's not far," said Katy.

"All right," said Pat. "Just a quick look. I mustn't stay long. I have such a lot of letters today."

Pat put his full bag of letters down, next to baby Paul, and went to see the pony.

The pony was just as lovely as Katy and Tom had said. It trotted across the field to them, and they gave it an apple. Pat stroked it.

"She's a real beauty," said Pat. "But I'll have to be getting on with my letters, now."

Just as they were all going back into the house, they could hear Mrs Pottage saying, "Oh, no, Paul, what have you done?"

And what a sight they saw when they walked into the kitchen!

"Oh, no!" said Pat and Katy and Tom, together.

There was a great big jumbled pile of letters next to Paul, and Paul had one of them in his mouth. He had opened Pat's bag, and tipped all the letters out of it.

"I think he's trying to sort your letters for you," said Mrs Pottage. "Oh, I am sorry, Pat. That's with me having my nose in a book. What a jumble! Don't worry, Pat. We'll all help to sort them out for you. Won't take long, if Paul doesn't help."

Mrs Pottage lifted Paul off the floor, and put him in his high-chair. Then she gave him his milk.

13

"There," she said. "That'll keep him out of mischief while we sort these letters out. I don't think Pat can deliver them the way Paul's sorted them."

They spread the letters out on the carpet, making a pile for each person in Greendale. All went well, and they had nearly finished, when Katy said,

"Oh, look!"

At the bottom of the heap of letters was a little pile of torn-up paper. You could see scraps of writing on the paper, and one piece had half a stamp on it.

"He's torn up a letter," said Mrs Pottage. "Oh dear. I wonder if it's an important one."

"We can fit it together," said Katy.

"Like a jigsaw puzzle," said Tom.

"Don't worry, Pat," said Katy. "We're good at jigsaws. We'll do it in a jiff."

Mrs Pottage gathered all the pieces carefully, and put them on the table. They all gathered round and began to sort out the torn pieces of letter.

"It says something about coming on a visit, here," said Tom.

"You're not supposed to read other people's letters," said Mrs Pottage.

"We can't sort it out without reading it," said Katy. "What does this bit say, mum?"

"Hm, can't make it out. Something about a pig, I think. But never mind what it says. Just fit the bits together. I wonder who it's for? They're not going to be very pleased to get their letter in tiny pieces."

What a time they had, fitting that letter together! They were getting on quite well, when Peter Fogg called. A puff of wind came in with him, and mixed all the pieces up again, so he stayed to help.

Then Granny Dryden popped in and said, "I'll give you a hand if I can only find my glasses."

But they were in none of her pockets. Then she emptied her handbag out on the table to try and find them, and some of the pieces of letter got mixed up with handbag things.

In the end, she sat down in the basket chair with a cup of tea.

"If that letter's for me," she said, you'll have to read it for me. I'd never be able to see it without my glasses."

The Reverend Timms came with the Parish Magazine, and he stayed to help.

"The Lord will guide us," he said. "I wonder if it's for me? It could be from my sister in Australia."

Then he spotted Mrs Pottage's new library books, and sat down to read one of them. He wasn't much help after that.

Miss Hubbard called in with a bottle of rhubarb wine. When she saw what they were doing, she said,

"Goodness me, you're doing it all wrong. Look here, I'll show you how to do it; you want to put them like this . . ."

Then someone jogged her elbow, and
the pieces got all mixed up again. She was
so cross that she had to sit down with a
cup of tea, as well.

Then baby Paul began to cry, and Mrs Pottage had to pick him up and nurse him till he went to sleep, so she couldn't help with the letter.

"Oh dear," she said, "we're not getting on very well, are we? And here's poor Pat getting later and later with his deliveries."

It was true. There were so many people in that kitchen now, some helping and some not, that they were getting in each other's way. The letter still wasn't sorted out.

Sam Waldron came in with a big box of groceries.

"Where shall I put this?" he said. "Hello, are you playing a game? Who's winning? Ooh, excuse me, this is heavy, I'll have to put it down."

And he put the box on the table, with quite a few pieces of letter under it. When he moved the box to the washing machine top, quite a lot of small leaves, bits of onion skin, and squashed peas, had joined the pieces of letter to be sorted. It might be that parts of the letter had stuck to the bottom of the box, too.

There was another knock at the door.

"Now who can that be?" said Mrs Pottage. "We'll have all Greendale here, soon."

It was Dorothy Thompson.

"Good morning," she said, "I've brought you two jars of my lemon cheese. I just made it yesterday. It's delicious. You must try it. It's lovely on toast."

So she had to come in. And now more tea had to be made, and lots and lots of toast, so that everyone could try the lemon cheese. Dorothy Thompson's lemon cheese was famous all over Greendale, and even in Pencaster. It was as delicious as it always was. The trouble is that you cannot eat toast and lemon

cheese without getting sticky fingers, so that now the pieces of letter began to stick to people's fingers. When they wanted to put a piece of letter down in the place where it just fitted, they found that they couldn't. They had to shake their hands to get the paper off, and then it flew just anywhere.

"I think we'd better all go and wash our hands," said Mrs Pottage. "We'll never do it whilst we're all sticky. Thank you Dorothy, just one more piece, then."

So then they all had to wait their turn at the sink, or in the bathroom, to get unstickied.

Whilst they were in the bathroom,
Katy and Tom thought they would like to
sail their boats in the bath, so they didn't
do any more sorting after that.

34

Then came another knock at the door.

"I'm going to lock that door," said Mrs Pottage.

But it was Ted Glen, with the grandfather clock. Mrs Pottage had been waiting years for Ted to mend that clock, so she certainly wasn't going to ask him to come another day with it. It might be years and years before he brought it again. Everyone had to move to make room for the clock to be carried in, it was so big.

Even the table had to be lifted out of the way. It was then that it tipped right over, and spilt all the pieces of letter on the floor!

"What's all that paper on the floor?" said Ted.

"That," said Pat, "is one of my letters. We've been trying half the morning to get it fitted together."

"Oh, no it's not! Well, it is, but it's my letter as well!" cried Mrs Pottage, kneeling on the floor, looking at a bigger piece of paper. "Look! I saw this when we moved the table. It has my name on it. And I know the writing. It was his Nanna's letter that Paul tore up."

"What you need now is a spot of glue," said Ted.

He took a big tube of glue out of his overall pocket.

"And a nice piece of card. Here, the lid of this grocery box will do. Then, if you spread some glue on the card, like this, you can stick the pieces of letter down as you find them. That way, they'll not keep blowing away, or getting dropped, or sticking to fingers, or whatever."

"Ted," said Pat, "you're a genius."

Doing what Ted had told them, they soon had the letter pieced together, and now Mrs Pottage could read it at last.

"Oh!" she said. "Nanna's coming to tea to-morrow, and bringing Auntie Kate, Auntie Pamela and Great Aunt Sylvia.

Gracious me, I haven't seen all the aunts at once for years and years. I'll have to make a cake, and scones, and biscuits, and fresh bread. I'm sorry folks! I'll have to speed you on your way. Can't have a kitchen full of visitors when I'm baking."

"And I'll have to be on my way with all these letters," said Pat. "It's a good thing there's only one letter like that."

"I'm glad it was mine that he tore up," said Mrs Pottage, "but I'm sorry we have made you so late, Pat."

"Oh, it's all right," said Pat. "I'll manage. I always do, whatever happens. The Greendale folk will understand."

One by one, they all went on their way,
leaving Mrs Pottage to get her kitchen to
rights, and make a start on the baking.

The next day, after the aunts had been to tea, Mrs Pottage called round at Pat's house. She brought a big tin of cakes, and scones, and home-made biscuits. (Anyone who has tasted Mrs Pottage's baking will know what a treat that was. She wins prizes for her cakes at Pencaster Show every single year.)

"This is just to make up for all that trouble you had with the letters," she said.

"Delicious," said Pat. "Thank you very much."

Pat, and Sara, and young Julian, had a real feast with that tin of good things. It lasted for days.

"I'll tell you what," said Sara. "Next time my mum sends a letter, I'll save it. Then you can give it to Paul. You never know. He might tear it up."